Stories for Five-Year-Olds

Other Story Collections in this Series:

Stories for
Five-Year-Olds

by
Chris Powling,
Penny Speller,
Julia Jarman,
Leon Rosselson,
Wendy Eyton
and Pat Thomson

Illustrated by George Buchanan

This book is set in 17pt Plantin

Printed in Great Britain by

HarperCollins Manufacturing, Glasgow

CONTENTS

THE CONTEST
NOT TO BE QUEEN
by Chris Powling

King Zap's beard was **ENORMOUS**.
It floated down from his face,
across his chest, out of his lap, round
his knees and over his feet like a drift
of the freshest, softest snow. People

shivered the instant they saw it.

"With a beard like that," they said,

"King Zap must be so old, he's ancient!"

King Zap agreed with them.

"Listen to me, Prime Minister," he grumbled. "My beard is so long and so white, how can I go on being king? Why, whenever I nod my head these days I have to lie down at once for a rest. And shaking my head is even worse – it takes me hours and hours to get my breath back! The time has come for me to retire. One of my daughters must take my place."

"One of your daughters, your majesty?"

"That's right."

"But your majesty ..."

"Yes?"

The Prime Minister took a deep breath.

"Don't you remember, your majesty?" he said. "We had this problem the last time you wanted to retire. Your three daughters are triplets. They're exactly the same age, look exactly alike and wear exactly the same clothes. No one can tell which is which – it's like trying to sort out three peas in a pod. What's more, not one of them wants to be Queen."

"Why not?" asked the King.

"They say being Queen is boring, your majesty. Compared with their own jobs, that is."

"Their own jobs? What jobs?"

The Prime Minister sighed. He'd

told the King this already, over and over again, but he didn't dare say so. "Princess Onesy is a hairdresser," he explained. "Princess Twosy is a blacksmith. And Princess Threesy is a swordfighter."

"A swordfighter, a blacksmith and a hairdresser?" said the King. "Are those better jobs than being Queen?"

"That's what they say, your majesty – especially since they're so good at what they do. Why, Princess Onesy is the finest hairdresser there's ever been, Princess Twosy is the finest blacksmith there's ever been ..."

"... and I suppose Princess Threesy is the finest swordfighter there's ever been," said the King. "That's the trouble with my three daughters –

they hate being beaten by anyone. The country can't have three queens, Prime Minister. And they'll never agree to take turns. How on earth can I retire if I can't choose which princess is to follow me?"

"That's a good question, your majesty."

"Then you'd better find a good answer, hadn't you. Otherwise I may look for someone new to do your job."

This was enough for the Prime Minister, you can bet. He began to think hard.

Next day he came up with a plan. When King Zap heard the details, he beamed with delight.

"Well done, Prime Minister! Tell

everyone in the palace to meet me out on the royal patio straight away. And fetch the three princesses at once. We'll begin the contest as soon as they arrive."

The contest?

What contest was this?

Princess Onesy, Princess Twosy and Princess Threesy were furious when they found out. "You mean we've got to show how good we are at our jobs?" they protested. "In front of all these people. And the one who's best becomes Queen? That's ridiculous! None of us wants to be Queen. So why should we even try?"

The Prime Minister smiled craftily. "You've got to try," he said, "because it's not the one who's the best who becomes Queen. It's the one who's the worst. If you want to keep the job you've got, you'd better make sure you're the first or second."

"You mean the one who's last becomes Queen?" said Princess Onesy.

"That's not fair," said Princess Twosy.

"We've been tricked!" said Princess Threesy.

They couldn't do a thing about it, though … not out there on the royal patio, surrounded by all the Lords and Ladies of the court, with their very own father smiling from deep in his beard.

"Let the Contest begin!" announced the Prime Minister.

Princess Onesy stepped forward. "Watch this, Daddy-your-majesty," she said.

Lifting a couple of fingers to her lips, she whistled across the royal park.

Was it a rabbit that answered her call? Or a dog?

It was both! Running full-pelt across the royal grass came a baby rabbit only a split-second ahead of a snapping, barking hound. As they swerved round Princess Onesy's feet, she went to work.

SNIP! SNIP! SNIP! went her scissors on rabbity whiskers and rabbity tail.

ATISHOO! went the hound as it sniffed the fluff she'd cut off.

LIPPETY-LIPPETY-LIPPETY!
went the extra-fast, extra-light rabbit
as it vanished in the trees up ahead.

Princess Onesy bowed to the King.
"See that, Daddy-your-majesty?" she
said. "My scissors saved the rabbit's
life. Don't worry, its whiskers and tail
will soon grow back again. Now you
know why people call me the niftiest
hairdresser who's ever been."

"I'll say," her dad gasped.

As the clapping and cheering died
down, Princess Twosy stepped
forward. "Watch this, Daddy-your-
majesty," she said.

From her pocket she took a tiny
hammer-and-tongs, a tiny anvil, a
tiny fire stuffed with a tiny pile of iron
already red-hot … and a bluebottle.

Everything was so tiny – especially the bluebottle – the King could hardly see what she was up to.

HISSSSSSS!!!!! went the iron in the fire.

DINKY-DINK, DINKY-DINK, DINKY-DINK! went the hammer and tongs on the anvil.

BUZZ-BUZZ-BUZZ! went the bluebottle.

Carefully, Princess Twosy put the bluebottle down on the royal patio. "Giddy-up!" she said.

CLIP-CLOP, CLIP-CLOP, CLIP-CLOP, CLIP-CLOP came the sound of tiny, iron feet.

Princess Twosy bowed to the King. "See that, Daddy-your-majesty?" she said. "A set of horse-shoes so small they fit a bluebottle … now you know why people call me the niftiest blacksmith there's ever been."

"I'll say," her dad gaped.

As soon as the clapping and cheering died down, Princess Threesy stepped forward. "Watch this, Daddy-your-majesty," she said.

With her thin, glittery sword she pointed upwards.

High over the royal patio hung a small black cloud. Even as they watched, a single raindrop plunged down. It would have splashed on the head of King Zap himself if Princess Threesy hadn't picked it with her sword.

PING!

Down fell a second raindrop … and

a third.

PING! PING!

Next came a shower.

PING! PING! PING! PING!
PING!

Finally, the whole cloud burst.

PING! PING! PING! PING!
PING! PING! PING! PING!

Everyone was drenched – the Prime
Minister, the Lords and Ladies, the
three Princesses ... everyone, that is,
apart from King Zap. Stabbing so fast
at raindrops that she was blurry,
Princess Threesy kept him dry as a
bone. "See that Daddy-your-
majesty?" she said. "A blade can be
better than a brolly if it's quick
enough. Now you know why people
call me the niftiest swordfighter

there's ever been."

"I'll say," her dad goggled.

By the time the rain stopped and Princess Threesy had bowed to the King, there was pandemonium on the patio. Wet as they were, the lords and ladies couldn't stop clapping and cheering. But who did they think had done best?

Some shouted for Princess Onesy.

Some shouted for Princess Twosy.

Some shouted for Princess Threesy.

Most of them, though – easily most of them – shouted for all three Princesses together. "Everyone's a winner!" they cried. "No one deserves to lose! Isn't that right, your majesty?"

"Quite right," groaned King Zap.

Gloomily, he looked at the Prime Minister. Even more gloomily, the Prime Minister looked back at him. But King Zap had a kind heart after all. "I can't blame you, Prime Minister," he said. "Who could've guessed the Contest would be a dead heat? I'll just have to go on being King, I suppose – despite this long, white beard of mine dragging me down."

"Just a moment," said Princess Onesy.

"We can do something about that," said Princess Twosy.

"You should have asked us in the first place," said Princess Threesy.

CLINKETTY-CLINK! went Twosy's hammer and tongs as they

sharpened Onesy's scissors.

ZIPPETTY-ZIP! went Onesy's scissors as she trimmed the royal cheeks till they were as smooth as a baby's bottom.

Before King Zap could say a word it was over.

The Court held its breath.

Slowly, rubbing a face so unhairy he could hardly believe it was his, the King stood up from his throne. He nodded his head. Then he shook his head. He stared at the snowy whiteness all round him.

"I feel younger," he said. "Much, much younger! Come to think of it, I don't feel old at all now – so who needs to retire? I might as well go on being King!"

Which he did, thank goodness. For years and years and years.

By then, of course, Princess Onesy, Twosy and Threesy were ready to take turns at being Queen. I'd love to say which of them was best at it but I'm afraid that isn't possible. You see, since they were exactly the same age, looked exactly alike and wore exactly the same clothes, no one could ever tell.

SAM'S MYSTERY GIFT
by Penny Speller

Plop. A bright pink envelope landed
on the doormat. Sam gazed at the
gold writing and picked it up.

"Look at this letter," he said.

"It's rubbish. Throw it away," said
his mum on her way past.

But Sam liked the look of the

envelope. He ripped it open and unfolded the papers inside. He found pages of writing which he couldn't read and pictures of cars, computers and televisions. There were some people with smiling faces beside them. A postcard fell to the floor. It had W-I-N in big bold letters and P-R-I-Z-E-S in even bigger letters.

"We might have won something," Sam called to his mother.

"No chance," she shouted back. "It's all to make you buy something. No one ever wins. Throw it in the bin."

"No way," thought Sam and he carefully wrote his name on the postcard together with his address and put it in his pocket. After breakfast he walked to school with his mum and on the way he slipped the postcard into a letterbox.

Two days later it was Saturday. Sam was down to breakfast later than usual.

"Oh, there's the doorbell," called his mum. "I'm just doing some cooking. Can you answer it for me, Sam."

Sam opened the door.

"Sam Sidney Sullivan?" It was the postman. He was holding a clipboard and a cardboard box.

"What?" asked Sam.

"Sign this," he said and thrust the clipboard towards Sam. "All recipients must sign on delivery."

"Am I a recipient?" asked Sam.

"Says so here," said the postman. "So hurry up. I've got other prizes to deliver."

"What prizes?" asked Sam and signed his name.

"Six months' supply of Sparkling Fresh toothpaste and one mystery gift," the postman read from his clipboard.

"What mystery gift?" asked Sam.

The postman stood back.

"This 'ere 'ippopotamus." He waved to a round grey animal standing behind him. It was about the size of a large dog.

"But I can't take that," gasped Sam. "Mum'll go mad."

"That's your problem," said the

man. "Done my bit." He marched back to his van. "Tell her it's only a pygmy 'ippo," he called back. "Won't get any bigger."

"I don't think she'll like it big or small," thought Sam and he stared at the hippopotamus. Although its skin was smooth, it bulged in places. It looked like a teddy bear that wasn't stuffed properly. It had two fat, yellow teeth sticking out either side of its mouth. Sam couldn't be sure, but he thought he could see a smile in the way it was looking. He gulped and began to wish he had thrown that envelope away.

The hippo lifted its head slightly.

"I will only eat the very freshest young leaves," it said. "Nothing brown or wilted."

"Did you speak?" Sam asked.

"Only the freshest," he went on. "And I must have a cool muddy river."

"My mum hates mud," said Sam. "And as for a river …"

"A deep pond would suffice," said the hippo. "Not too small, plenty of pondweed and no goldfish – I can't abide the tickling."

"You'd better come in," said Sam. He was trying to think where he could find a pond.

The hippo plodded obediently into the hall as if it were an old friend who'd come to tea. Sam put the box of toothpaste down and carefully shut the front door so as not to alert his mum.

"Would you like to try the

toothpaste?" he asked.

"Leaves," said the hippo. It was looking at a vase of flowers on the window sill. "And I'm ready for the pond. My skin feels dry."

"What about a bath?" asked Sam. "That's wet."

"You really should have been better prepared," moaned the hippo.

"It's upstairs," said Sam. He looked at the hippo's short fat legs. "I'll help you."

The hippo put its feet on the bottom step and wobbled. Its body shook like a big shiny jelly. Sam pushed and shoved against its bottom. The hippo's feet made a 'thump clunk' as he went and the bannister creaked as its round body squeezed past.

"What's all that noise?" called Sam's mum.

"Just me," said Sam. "Practising headstands."

"Well, stop it. You'll have the whole house down," she called back.

Sam shoved harder against the hippo's bottom.

"Mind where you're pushing," it complained.

"You shouldn't be so fat," puffed Sam as he reached the top step.

Sam had to heave the hippo into the bath. First he turned on the tap. Then he lifted the front feet up and pushed from the back so that the hippo tipped head first into the water.

It made a tremendous splash. Sam's T-shirt was soaked and the hippo bonked its nose on the tap as it slid forward. It sighed and ducked its head under the water so that only its eyes on the top of its head stayed dry. It looked around and spotted a fern on the window sill.

"That won't be enough for breakfast," it said. "I wouldn't even call it a snack."

"You can't have that," Sam was horrified. "It's my mum's. What about a lettuce." He ran down to the kitchen.

"What do you want for breakfast?" asked his mum.

"Lettuce," said Sam. His mum gave him a funny look and got one out of the fridge.

"You don't like lettuce," she said.

"I do now." Sam grabbed it from her. "I'll have it all and eat it upstairs." He rushed out before she could argue. When he reached the bathroom, the hippo had a suspicious green smudgy smile on his face. The fern looked a lot smaller.

"Here," said Sam. He produced the lettuce. The hippo chewed it up in seconds, and dropped bits into the bath which floated around his legs.

"I could eat ten of those," he said. "Fetch me another."

"I can't," said Sam. "There isn't any more."

The doorbell rang again.

"You get it," called his mum. "I'm just doing the washing-up."

33

Sam went to answer the door. It was the postman again.

"It's about the 'ippo," he said.

"What?" asked Sam.

"Been a mix up. Wrong delivery. I've got to have it back," he said.

"It's in the bath," said Sam. "I'll go and get it."

The hippo was still dribbling lettuce and dripping bath water as Sam pushed it back down the stairs.

"Wish you'd make your mind up," it grumbled.

"Here," said the postman. "You should've had this." He gave Sam a poster. Sam watched the hippo wobble back to the van and then he looked at his prize. It was a chart

about how to prevent tooth decay. "I'd rather have a hippopotamus," he thought and shut the door.

"Who was that?" asked his mum as she came out of the kitchen.

"Just the postman," said Sam. "I've won six months' supply of toothpaste."

"Goodness!" said Mum. "Whatever will the postman deliver next?"

SILLY GOOSE
by Julia Jarman

There was once a goose called
Griselda. She was a white goose, with
a beak as bright as a newly-washed
carrot. Her feet were orange too, but
paler. She lived by a pond, in the
middle of a park, in the middle of a

town called Puddley.

Every morning Griselda toured the park with her beak in the air.

"Look at me, I'm such a beautiful goose," she seemed to say.

And everyone looked, and smiled as she passed. Head high, tail low, her orange feet marched proudly forward and her white bottom rolled along behind. Pit pat wobble fat. Pit pat wobble.

Griselda was the only goose in Puddley Park, but sometimes she swam and dipped with the mallard ducks, their feathers brown and beige – dull and dingy, Griselda thought. And she raced the drakes, who were handsome in purple and glossy green.

Blotchy, thought Griselda.

It wasn't true. The fact was that Griselda couldn't see very well. Griselda should have worn glasses, but she thought they would hide her beautiful pale blue eyes. And so Griselda looked at the world as if through very muddy water.

And that's why she made her Very Silly Mistake.

Not seeing very well didn't matter very much, not while she stayed by the pond in the middle of the park, in the middle of the town called Puddley.

She had water.

She had food to eat.

She had reeds to sleep in when the sun slipped behind the trees in the corner of the park. And she had friends – if she had wanted them – for the birds and animals in Puddley Park loved her.

They loved her because she told them stories.

Every evening as the sky turned pink and then indigo, before they roosted or burrowed or bedded down, Griselda told them tales.

She told them of princesses and castles, of giants and dragons and faraway places, and of Very Clever Animals. Once upon a time, she said, there was a cat in boots who made a fortune for his master, a pig who outwitted a wolf, a homely hen who baked bread and a goose who laid a golden egg!

They were wonderful stories that filled the animals' dreams. So they loved Griselda and Griselda was content.

"I'm the most beautiful bird in the park," she thought. "I'm whiter than the washing on the park-keeper's line. My beak is brighter than the autumn leaves. There is no one to equal me."

And this made her feel very proud – and a little bit lonely.

When Winter came, visitors from Iceland and Alaska, from Russia, Sweden and Canada flew in, some in ones and twos, others in long skeins and V-formations. The pond froze and strange sounds filled the park, and exotic colours , though Griselda was too short-sighted to see these.

Pink-footed geese ink-inked noisily. Golden-eyed ducks k-k-k-karred, and diving ducks with red crests wheezed.

But most striking of all was a very handsome Canada Goose called Hank. His neck was black, his back was brown with white stripes. And he fell in love with Griselda.

Now Hank had a honk that stirred her, though she didn't much like what he said: "You need spectacles, Griselda."

But he was a good listener too. He loved Griselda's stories. He loved Griselda – but Griselda didn't love Hank.

"He's not handsome enough," she said to herself. "Not handsome enough for me."

All winter he wooed her. All winter she spurned him.

Then Spring came to the pond in the middle of the park in the middle of the town called Puddley. Buds fattened on the chestnut trees and burst into leaf. Frogs spawned, their jelly rich and wriggling with tiny tadpoles. Sparrows fought then mated and built neat nests in the hedges. Rooks quawked and quarked and heaped twigs on the tops of beech trees. Slim slugs left silver trails along the park benches.

And one day the winter visitors left. But not Hank. He stayed and brought Griselda gifts.

Meanwhile, the grass grew juicier.

Griselda watched. She felt a tingling in her light orange feet and a prickling in her feathers.

Hank honked but she didn't hear him.

"I want ..."

"I want ..."

Griselda wasn't sure what she wanted but she set off to find it, neck out-stretched, goose-stepping through the park.

She passed the statue of a famous general.

She passed the slide and round-about and swings.

She passed the gateposts as she left the park and stepped into the High Street.

"You're not tall enough," she said to the gatepost.

She passed the litter-bin.

"You're too small," she said.

She passed the pillar-box.

"And you're too fat – and red."

And then she saw him, by the side of a sign saying ROADWORKS AHEAD. But Griselda was short-sighted. She could not see the sign and she could not see ahead. She could see only him.

She thought he was the handsomest gander she had ever seen.

He was tall enough.

He was thin enough.

His beak was even brighter than hers. But best of all were his flashing eyes. One was red and one was green!

Griselda ogled him with her own blue eyes and honk-honked in a 'Do come closer' sort of way.

But he didn't come closer. He didn't move at all. But he did wink at her with his flashing green eye.

Passers-by stopped and stared. The road-menders stopped mending. Shop-keepers stood in their doorways and the workers in the bottle factory stuck their heads out of the window.

"What is that goose doing, staring at a traffic light?"

All through the day Griselda gazed – and all through the night – and all through the next day.

Only when the hunger in her stomach hurt much more than the

hunger in her heart did she think of food. And then she turned and pecked in an uninterested sort of way at the blades of grass which grew between the paving stones.

And then she gazed again.

Hank brought her choice morsels to eat, and tried to tell her of her mistake.

"You're only jealous," she said.

Nothing distracted her. Traffic rumbled by. Diggers clattered and banged. Cement mixers clonked and sloshed and whirred. Drills d... d... d... D... D...DEAFENED passers-by.

But Griselda stayed by her love.

Daily she grew thinner.

Until one day a lorry arrived.

Workmen jumped down, opened the tail-gate. Carefully, they lifted out a large round thing, carried it to the side of the road and fixed it on a pole. Then they took off the sacking wrapped round it.

At first it dazzled Griselda. It faced the sun and she couldn't see anything. She could only hear people.

"That'll be better. Safer now. Drivers will be able to see round that bend."

For the large round object was a mirror, a very big mirror like a magnifying glass. It was curved at the edges to show drivers what was coming round the corner.

Griselda pit patted up to it and stared. It showed Griselda –

GRISELDA!

"I'm HUGE and I've got an enormous fat beak with HOLES in it – like caves. And my mouth is all jagged at the edges. I'm UGLY."

And reflected in the mirror next to Griselda was not a handsome gander but a traffic light.

Her love was a traffic light!

"I'm silly," said Griselda miserably, "and ugly."

"You're not," honked Hank, "you're beautiful and VERY clever. Come back to the pond."

Griselda looked at Hank. He really was quite handsome. And he was very kind.

And so Griselda and Hank went back to the pond where all the other birds and animals were very pleased to see them together.

But most of all they were pleased to hear Griselda. For that night she told them stories again. She began with a new one. "There was once a very silly goose called Griselda… "

THE GIANT OF LILLIPUT LANE
by Leon Rosselson

Number thirteen Lilliput Lane was
where The Giant lived. Everyone
called him The Giant because
nobody knew his name. Perhaps he
didn't have one. The Giant lived with

his mother, a little grey-haired woman who looked after him. In fact, she did everything for him. He expected it. He was that sort of a giant.

"Mummy, bring me my slippers," called The Giant. And she did.

"Mummy, fry me fifteen rashers of bacon and seventeen eggs for my breakfast," ordered The Giant. And she did.

"Mummy, I want you to cut my toe nails for me," demanded The Giant. So she did.

She loved her son, Mrs Giant did.

One hot summer's day, The Giant lay in the long grass in the back garden. Mummy was fetching and carrying backwards and forwards from the garden to the house and from the house to the garden.

"I'm thirsty, Mummy," said The Giant. "Bring me some iced water."

Mummy trotted into the house and staggered out again carrying a barrel full of water which The Giant drained in an instant as if it was a mere thimbleful.

"Now I need my portable telephone," The Giant declared.

Mummy ran into the house to fetch his giant telephone. He was just beginning to dial an important telephone number when a brightly-coloured football sailed over the fence at the end of the garden, over the saplings, the giant ferns and the wild raspberry canes, over the hogweed, the cow parsley, the rosebay willowherb and the wild honeysuckle and …

"Catch it, Mummy," called The Giant, and with a sudden leap to her right, she did.

The Giant snatched the ball from her. "Mine," he said greedily. "Mine, mine, mine."

"I think, dear," Mummy said mildly, "it belongs to the twins in the house across the way."

"Inside this garden, all is mine," recited The Giant, "What's yours is mine, what's mine's my own, the birds, the bees, the butterflies, this tree, this ball, this telephone."

"If you say so, dear," Mummy agreed.

"I'm tired, Mummy," said The Giant. "Time for my afternoon nap." And using the football as a pillow, he lay down under the beech tree, while his mother fanned his face with a hogweed leaf and sang him a lullaby.

"Close your eyes, little one, time you were sleeping now, close your eyes, little one, nothing to fear. Go to sleep, honey bun, I will watch over you, fast asleep, honey bun, Mummy is here," she sang.

Soon The Giant's loud snores were making the beech tree shake and shudder.

Mummy looked at him fondly. "Isn't he lovely? Isn't he sweet?" she said to herself. "Look at my baby, fast asleep." Then she tiptoed into the house and settled down to knit her son a giant scarf for the winter.

In their neat and tidy garden, the twins were arguing.

"You kicked the ball over," said Henry. "So you should go and get it."

"You told me to kick it as hard as I could," said Henrietta. "So you should get it."

"Let's both go," they sang together.

But they didn't move. They were thinking about The Giant. He chops children up in a stew and eats them for his supper, they were both thinking.

"Are you scared?" asked Henry.

"I'm not scared if you're not scared," said Henrietta.

"I'm a bit scared," said Henry. "But it's my favourite football."

"And mine," said Henrietta.

"Giants!" said Henry. "They shouldn't be allowed."

Then they marched hand in hand to the fence at the end of their neat and tidy garden and wriggled through a small and secret hole into The Giant's garden. Suddenly, they were in a different world. Everything was tall and overgrown. There was a strange sweet smell in the air. Brightly coloured butterflies flitted past their noses. Fat furry bumble bees droned round their heads. Above them black and white house-martins were swooping and gliding, and they could hear the double trilling song of the thrush.

"It's like the jungle, said Henry. "Maybe we'll meet an elephant."

"How will we ever find the ball?" asked Henrietta.

"It went further on," Henry told her.

"Yes," said Henrietta. "I kicked it as hard as I could."

Soon they were peering through the dense tangle of wild flowers into the long grass where The Giant was sleeping. Their eyes opened wide.

"There's our ball," Henrietta whispered. "The Giant's sleeping on it."

"Oh, but he's big!" exclaimed Henry.

"That's because he's a giant,"

Henrietta said knowingly.

"How will we get the ball without waking him up?" said Henry.

"I'll hit him on the knee with this stick," said Henrietta, "and when he sits up ..."

"I'll grab the ball ..." said Henry.

"And we'll both run," they decided together.

They crawled through the long grass. Henry waited near The Giant's head, ready to snatch back the ball. Henrietta lifted up the stick and whacked The Giant on the knee. The Giant felt a tickle and sat up to scratch himself. Henry grabbed the ball. Henrietta dropped the stick. They both ran.

"Stop!" roared The Giant and

pulled them back.

"Help!" screamed the twins.

"How dare you steal my ball!" threatened The Giant.

"It's not your ball, it's our ball," said the twins. "We kicked it over the fence accidentally."

The Giant snatched back the ball. "Inside this garden all is mine," he recited. "What's yours is mine, what's mine's my own, the birds, the bees, the butterflies, this tree, this ball, this telephone."

"The birds and bees and butterflies aren't yours," said Henrietta. "They're everybody's. And that isn't your ball either."

"My mummy, too, belongs to me," added The Giant. "That is, she is my property."

"You're mean," said Henry.

"You're selfish," said Henrietta.

"You're the meanest, selfishest, nastiest, ugliest, horriblest giant we've ever seen," they shouted at him angrily.

The Giant was taken aback. The corners of his mouth began to turn down. His lower lip trembled. His shoulders hunched. A terrible sadness made his face sag. He rubbed his eyes with his rocky fists and let out a great cry. Giant tears rolled down his cheeks. Soon the twins were ankle deep in tears. They were amazed. They didn't know what to do.

"You don't know what it's like," sobbed The Giant. "It's no fun being a giant. Nobody likes me. Nobody comes to see me. Nobody talks to me. Nobody plays with me. Everybody tells nasty stories about me. I'm so lonely," he bawled.

The twins looked at each other. They were feeling sorry for The Giant. Such a big baby.

"We didn't mean it," they chorused "If you give us our ball back, we'll play with you."

The Giant stopped crying. He looked at them. "Will you?" he said. "Will you really?"

"Your garden's a lot more fun than ours," said Henrietta. "All those bees and butterflies."

"Lots of places to play hide-and-seek," said Henry.

The Giant smiled. Gently he

lobbed the ball to Henrietta who caught it and threw it to Henry. Henry hurled it with all his strength up to The Giant. He caught it one-handed and laughed. This strange sound brought his mother running into the garden. She had never heard her son laugh before.

"These are my friends," The Giant told her. "They've come to play with me."

"That's nice," said The Giant's mother. "That is nice." And she smiled contentedly.

THE PRANCING PRINCE
by Wendy Eyton

There was once a prince who loved to dress up in bright, colourful costumes and comb out his curly golden locks until they shone in the glow from the palace chandeliers. He liked to dance the minuet, and play croquet, but he was not interested in killing dragons, or chasing away monsters, or rescuing princesses, or anything like that.

"When I was your age," grumbled the king, "I would think nothing of killing seven dragons before breakfast."

"One, dear," put in the queen mildly. "And that was a very old one, and just before lunch."

The king picked up a copy of the Court Gazette and waved the pages of the newspaper at the prince, who was dangling cherries over his ears.

"A pearly-toothed princess has been locked inside a high tower by a wicked wizard," said the king. "He cast a spell on her several months ago. The tower is surrounded by a moat and drawbridge, and the moat is guarded by an immense fiery dragon."

"Dear, dear," murmured the queen, putting on her reading spectacles. "It says that to break the wizard's spell a brave prince must overcome the fiery dragon, cross the moat and vanquish the Green-Eyed Goggle that guards the door to the tower. Whatever do you suppose a green-eyed goggle is?"

The king did not know, but he was determined that the prince was going to find out.

"You will never be fit to rule my kingdom unless you kill a few dragons and rescue a few princesses," he told his son. "And this sounds as easy a first job as any."

And he told the prince to be up at dawn and ready to set out on his quest as soon as possible.

But the prince did not roll out of bed until eleven o'clock, and then he could not find a suit of armour to fit him.

"It's so ugly and so uncomfortable," he complained, clanking about the palace corridors. "I can't bend my knees and I can't bend my arms and I can't see where I'm going. Oh, drat the thing."

And he threw off every bit of armour and dressed himself most carefully in the latest craze in tights, with one of his legs covered in bright red wool and the other in bright yellow. Then he put on a doublet and shoes of softest leather, with toes twelve inches long that curled up at the ends, mounted his horse with some difficulty and rode out of the palace gates.

To reach the tower where the princess was held prisoner, the prince had to cross many miles of rolling countryside. He was not a good horseman at the best of times, but to urge the animal on was nearly impossible, because he was wearing such silly shoes. And the horse refused to jump over ditches and wanted to stop at every stream for a long, cool drink and at every hedgerow for a tasty nibble.

At last the prince, utterly fed up, climbed off his horse and gave it a slap on the rump that sent it cantering back to the palace. But after half an hour he wished he had not done so, for the soft rolling hillside gave way to rough moorland, and the gorse and bracken pricked the prince's feet through his soft leather shoes, and tore his tights until they hung in shreds.

Complaining and muttering, the prince, at long last, spied in the distance a high, turreted tower, surrounded by a shining moat. And there, sure enough, guarding the drawbridge, was a dragon. The newspaper had exaggerated, as usual, and the dragon was not all that immense, but he was quite fiery, and the grass beneath his feet was scorched black and brown.

"Hold it!" cried the prince in a quavering voice and then, remembering that he had not brought any weapon, was about to run.

But at the sight of him the dragon started to roar, not with anger but with laughter, and he laughed so much that salty tears ran in rivulets down his hoary cheeks and, in no time at all, the dragon's fiery breath had fizzled into a single plume of thin, grey smoke and disappeared. Then the dragon lumbered away from the blackened grass at his feet, sniffed at the sweeter grass in the meadow and started munching it. He took no more notice of the prince, who darted round behind him and managed to lower the drawbridge, but not without hurting his back and breaking his fingernails, which made him very cross.

The Green-Eyed Goggle, that guarded the tower door, was every bit as hideous as could be expected. It had one huge eye in the centre of its forehead, and the eye was green and glaring with thousands of different sides to it the way a fly's eye has. Legend says that if the Green-Eyed Goggle stared at you for sixty seconds you would turn to stone for the next ten years – and, certainly, there were stone statues all over the place.

The prince stood his ground and raised his eyeglass to look at the goggle, not because he was brave, but because he was short-sighted and had not received the full impact of the hideous thing. But the Goggle was fascinated by the eyeglass, that hung on a gold chain around the prince's neck, and it made all sorts of repulsive sounds like "Gimme–GimmeGimme," and put out its knobbly fist. The prince held on to the eyeglass, because he could not understand goggle language, but the creature snatched the glass and chain away from him, and threw down an iron key in exchange.

While the Goggle played with the eyeglass, the prince unlocked the door of the tower with the heavy iron key, puffing at the stiffness of it, and ran up the stone steps inside the tower – hundreds and hundreds of them – until he thought his knees would cave in.

The princess had lovely pearly teeth it is true, but she showed them in an unfriendly scowl when the prince, panting and dishevelled, burst through her chamber door. Collapsing on to a silk-fringed stool, the prince explained that he had come a long way and faced many dangers to rescue her from the wizard's spell.

"But I can't come yet," pouted the princess, who was busy with her embroidery frame. "There's still a leaf and a bluebird to do."

"Well, bring the embroidery with you," urged the prince. "We must get away before the dragon stops eating grass and the Goggle gets tired of its new plaything."

He led the princess gently to the top of the stairs, but after going down two or three steps, she protested so much about how steep they were and how slippery they were, and how her dress was getting dirty, that he had to take her back to the tower, past the Goggle, who was looking through the glass with the hundredth side of its great eye – and up to the dragon to ask if he would do him a favour.

"Anything, dear chap," said the

dragon. "It was so good of you to put my fire out. The grass hasn't tasted so fresh for years."

So he allowed the prince to climb on to his back, and they rose up, up into the air to rescue the princess from her pointed turret window.

But when the princess saw the great beast flapping about outside, she ran to the other end of the chamber, pressed herself against the wall and screamed at the prince that she liked living in a tower and working on her embroidery frame, and just wanted to be left alone.

So the prince went for a ride around the country on the dragon's back instead, and enjoyed it so much that he did not return home for three years.

In the meantime, his younger brother, who loved killing dragons, and hated croquet and dressing up, also went in search of the princess.

He spurred his horse across the hills and moorland, swam the width of the moat, chased away the Green-Eyed Goggle and leapt up the steps of the tower three and four at a time.

And when he saw the princess, he threw her over his shoulder, carried her back to the palace and married her before she had time to argue.

So, perhaps everything ended happily, after all.

NEIGHBOURS
by Pat Thomson

George sprang up to the top of the
fence, his claws rattling on the wood.
One black cat.

Bluebell sprang up beside him, then
they both dropped into the next
garden. Two black cats.

They lashed their tails once or twice and stalked up and down a little, just in case any other cat had dared come into their jungle. The next door house had been empty for a long time so they came every day to prowl among the bushes.

They sat down. George stretched in the sun and blinked. Bluebell licked her smooth black fur. A peaceful morning in the sun, that was what George and Bluebell liked.

My goodness! What was that? They sat up sharply and twitched their ears.

"Is it that screeching Siamese from two doors down?" growled George.

"No. Maybe it's that howling hunting dog from the corner house," said Bluebell.

"I know what it is," said George, "It's a human's kitten."

"Then the house isn't empty any more," replied Bluebell and they both got up and padded over to a window. They jumped on to the stone sill and stared in.

Inside the house, a little girl was not having her breakfast. Her mother looked tired and cross. Cardboard boxes were scattered over the kitchen floor. Things were half unpacked. The little girl took no notice of any of this. She just sat at the table and cried.

"Don't you want any breakfast?" asked the mother.

"No, no, no!" shouted the little girl and she pushed her plate away so hard, it nearly fell on the floor.

Bluebell hissed a little. "Her mother should pick her up by the scruff of her neck and put her back in her basket," she said.

"It will take a long time to lick that kitten clean," observed George.

The mother started to tidy up. "I think we brought the wrong little girl with us to the new house," said the mother. "You're not my nice little Anna today, are you?"

"No," said the little girl and she sniffed loudly.

"Don't you like our lovely new house and garden?"

"No!" She was shouting even louder and started to cry all over again.

"But you like your new little room, don't you? Of course you do!"

"NO," shouted the little girl and she cried even more.

"Anna, whatever's the matter?" asked her mother.

"I want to GO HOME," and she shouted so loudly, the windows rattled.

"Well," said Bluebell, twitching her tail, "I've never seen anything like it. She needs a firm paw, that one."

"She's unhappy," said George. "She's missing her old home. I ran away once, you know."

"Never!" exclaimed Bluebell.

"It was before you came. We moved here and I wanted to go back to the old house. They buttered my paws. That's supposed to make you feel at home. That's what they say, anyway.

But I didn't want to feel at home here so I walked up and down on their new carpet to punish them. It made a terrible mess."

He purred, remembering.

"But you soon grew to like it here, didn't you?" asked Bluebell.

"I discovered the garden. This garden."

They jumped down and began to explore as they did every morning. First, they sharpened their claws on the trunk of the tall lime tree. Then they walked over to a large, straggly lavender bush. There were bees all over it. George batted it with his paw.

"You'll do that once too often," observed Bluebell. "Mind your own business and the bees will mind theirs."

They strolled over to the wide, flat stone they sat on every day. It was warmed by the sun and they stayed there a little.

Then they went past the tangle of ivy on the wall. Bluebell stood on her hind legs and looked into the tangle. "The young birds have gone," she said.

"We musn't catch them, anyway," said George. "Everyone gets too cross." But he licked his lips all the same.

They went to see if there was anything interesting in the vegetable garden. It was all overgrown, but George ate some grass and chased a butterfly.

Then they went to their favourite

place. One behind the other, they crossed the garden path and walked among the shrubs and bushes. One after the other, they slipped under a laurel bush and lay down in the shade. It was a cool, green cave with a bed of dry leaves.

George stretched out and closed his eyes. Bluebell lay full length and washed her front paws from time to time.

"This would be very nice," said George, "if …"

"If it wasn't for the human kitten," finished Bluebell.

"Exactly," said George, putting his nose down and his paws over his ears. "I can hear it from here."

"Come along." Bluebell sprang up.

"We must do something about it."

"Must we?" asked George reluctantly.

"Certainly, George," said Bluebell, sternly. "We won't get any peace until we do."

They shook the dry leaves out of their fur and walked back to the house.

Perched on the window sill, the two black cats stared in again. The mother looked even more tired. She was trying to unpack while the little girl pulled at her skirt.

"Shall I unpack your toys?" the mother was saying.

"No!" shouted the little girl.

"Oh my!" said Bluebell.

"I know. We'll bake a nice cake," suggested the mother.

"No!" shouted the little girl.

"Shocking!" exclaimed Bluebell.

"Then you had better go to bed," said the mother suddenly standing up very straight.

"No, no, no!" shouted the little girl.

"Gracious!" said Bluebell. "Will its mother bite it?"

George sighed, but as he looked into the kitchen, the little girl turned round and stopped crying at once. She was staring straight at George and Bluebell and they stared back.

"Oh," she said, and was very quiet.

"They must have come from next door," said the mother, and the little girl managed to smile and ran to open the kitchen door.

Bluebell and George jumped down and went to meet her. They stalked up and down in an important way and kept their tails stiff so that the little girl could stroke them. Then they strolled off towards the garden. The mother stood watching at the door but the little girl followed them.

"Look, Mummy," she called, "there are claw marks on this tree. It's their sharpening tree."

They took her over to the lavender bush and Anna watched the furry bees hang on the flower heads. Her mother came to see and picked a flower.

"Smell it, Anna," she said. "Isn't it lovely? We'll dry some to remember the summer in the cold of winter."

But Anna had run over to the wide, flat stone. She sat on it and it was just the right size for one small girl with a black cat on either side of her.

When Bluebell went to explore the ivy, Anna stood on tiptoe to see what she was after.

"It's a nest," she told her mother. "A bird's nest in this garden."

"Good," said her mother. "We'll watch next spring. The birds might come again. And look, this is the old vegetable garden."

"Can I have a garden of my own?" asked Anna and she began to think what she might grow.

"The cats have disappeared," said the mother, but Anna had seen a tail under the laurel bush. She bent down and crawled under the low branches.

"Now you've disappeared," said the mother and Anna began to laugh.

"Can't you see me?" asked the bush. "There's a little house under here, with a carpet of brown leaves and a green ceiling." Then all the leaves shook and she scrambled out.

"Quickly, Mummy," said Anna, "help me unpack my tea-set. I'm going to have a house under the bush with the two black cats."

Anna played in her treehouse all the morning. Bluebell sniffed everything she was offered but she would not drink the water in the tea cups. She did eat the biscuit crumbs from the plates. George just purred and swished his tail and went for long walks.

When Anna was called in, the cats went to her door with her, then they strolled back to the fence.

"The human kitten is happy now," said George. "It has stopped wailing and howling, thank goodness."

"Yes, indeed," said Bluebell. "A mewling kitten is a great trial. I should know, having had twelve of my own. We'll come again tomorrow."

"She likes her new house, I think. She likes the garden, anyway," and George sprang at the fence.

"I think she does," agreed Bluebell, following him. They both dropped into their own garden. "They won't have to butter her paws after all!"